UP THE WALL

by Nicholas Heller

Greenwillow Books New York

FOR WOODY

Watercolor paints and a black pen line
were used for the full-color art.
The text type is ITC Carnese Text.

a division of William Morrow & Company, Inc.,
1350 Avenue of the Americas, New York, NY 10019.
Printed in Singapore by Tien Wah Press
First Edition   10 9 8 7 6 5 4 3 2 1

Library of Congress
Cataloging-in-Publication Data

Heller, Nicholas.
Up the wall / by Nicholas Heller.
       p.   cm.
Summary: When his family chase a boy
away while they are working, he packs his
food and toys, calls his dog, and walks
up the wall to the ceiling, where he can
hang around doing just as he likes.
ISBN 0-688-10633-1
ISBN 0-688-10634-X (lib.)
[1. Play — Fiction. 2. Fantasy.]
I. Title.   PZ7.H37426Up   1992
[E] — dc20
91-14783   CIP   AC

If I can't play in here
because my mother is working,

and I can't play in there
because my father is reading,

and my sister says, "Scram!
You're a boy — you can't be here,"

I fill a big bag with toys

and some food.

Then I call the dog,
and we walk up the wall

to the ceiling,
where there's plenty of space!

We skate around the living room

and bowl in the hall.

The house is ours.
We make lots of noise.

We play tag in the dining room

and jump through doors.

When we're hungry, we eat
(and we make a big mess).

If we're sleepy,
we nap in a doorway.

I lay train tracks in the kitchen,

build a castle in the bathroom.

I don't have to wash —
there's no sink and no tub here.

And I don't have to put things away.

But when suppertime comes —

YIPPEE!

"Where have you been all day long?"
they ask me.

"Just hanging around," I reply.